Light Remains
Three Stories

A.C. Fuller

Cover design by Yosbe Design

A.C. Fuller Books

Hansville, Washington

www.acfuller.com

ISBN: 154245879X
ISBN-13: 978-1542458795

OTHER BOOKS BY A.C. FULLER

The Cutline

The Anonymous Source

The Inverted Pyramid

DEDICATION

.

To my wife, Amanda, whose enthusiasm for my
stories makes them come to life.

CONTENTS

Transit umbra, lux permanet

Shadow passes, light remains.

CAN YOU HEAR ME NOW?

Seattle
Sunday, 6 AM

Survivors of near-death experiences often report some version of the same occurrence: their lives flashing before their eyes. Some describe a bodily sensation, like they are actually *reliving* every emotion and physical sensation they've ever experienced. Others see every instant passing through their mind on fast forward, starting at birth and ending in the moment they are about to die. For some, the process takes hours. For others, it's instantaneous. Some people even have guides who walk them through the journey.

Don't buy it?

Me neither, and not just because I'm a cynical engineer. Just think about what it would mean. If every memory—*every moment*—passes through you right before you die, that means that every moment is *remembered*. Maybe not consciously, but if it is able to flash through before you die, that means it's there, stored somehow, right now. Every moment of your life.

I always assumed that the eight-million Americans who have reported this were full of it. That they were—at best—hallucinating and—at worst—making it up after escaping death, partially to give the event meaning, but mostly to remind themselves and the rest of us to appreciate life.

It's what I assumed, that is, until the day I lost my iPhone.

It started when I rolled out of bed to get a glass of water, groggy but not hungover. The night before I'd had just the right number of pints at the local pub, The Lion's Breath. No, I'm not British, but yes, I *am* a pretentious asshole. I drink *pints* of ale and lager, sometimes even cider, I eat bangers and mash and fish and chips, and I call it a pub because that's what it's called.

I drank my water in the kitchen and looked around for my phone: kitchen counter, bedside table, jacket pockets. I checked the sofa cushions even though I couldn't remember whether I'd sat there the night before. I slid back into bed and ran my hands over the sheets and under the pillow, then looked in the crack of the bed frame. Nothing.

That's when *The Feeling* first hit me.

I design the home buttons on cell phones, the little round one you press a thousand times a day as you stare down, waiting for the magic to happen. If you're lucky, you just rest your thumb on it and the fingerprint technology does the rest. I helped come up with that, though I don't actually work for Apple or Samsung or any of the big guys. I work for one of the dozen companies to which they subcontract minor aspects of button design. At the office, we work to make every aspect of the phone fill you with feelings of connection and love. We want the phone to become an extension of your body, an extension of or even a *magnification* of your consciousness. A part of you.

So how do we know if we've succeeded? We know because, when you misplace your phone, you get The Feeling. Trust me, we designed it that way.

But as I rolled back into my bed at six in the morning, I was starting to feel it, too.

As it often does, The Feeling started as a vague thought: *What's missing?* But it quickly morphed into a series of more-specific notions. Someone may have commented on my Facebook post. Important tweets might be appearing and getting buried by other tweets before I have a chance to read them. How will I check the score in the Mariners game? Most importantly, I could be missing an important text. Maybe from Maria, the attractive, single, black-haired grad student I vaguely remembered exchanging numbers with the night before.

From there, The Feeling developed quickly: uncertainty, disconnection, frustration, a sense that I'd been untethered, like a piece of driftwood being carried out into the ocean. Just as we'd designed it to, the darkness descended quickly.

As I stared up at the ceiling, I actually thought *oh-holy-hell-my-life-is-over.* I was overcome with a sense of emptiness, and it brought with it the memories of my life, flooding in to fill the void. I won't say it was *all* the moments, but it damn sure seemed like most of them. A movie of my thirty-four years, playing at 100x speed, slowing down slightly from time to time so I could catch a glimpse of some of the moments.

Lying to my mom about losing my baseball glove, finding a dollar on the street and hiding it in the waistband of my underwear so my dad wouldn't accuse me of stealing it, Suzy Johnson grabbing my cupcake at my fourth birthday party, my Uber driver from last night, his yellow teeth and crooked smile. And there were smells, too: the sweet grass at Safeco Field, my dad's oily t-shirts in the garage, the dustiness of my first car.

I pulled the blankets over my head, determined to catch a few more hours of sleep. I knew I'd find my phone when I woke up and, as I nodded off, I thought back to my last yoga class and took five deep breaths.

I'd helped design this feeling, and I *wasn't* going to be taken away by it.

9 AM

Sometimes I like to take little breaks from my phone to show that I'm not an addict. To prove to myself that our design team's efforts have *not* worked on me.

So when I stepped out of bed onto my gleaming wood floors, sun streaming through the curtains announcing a beautiful summer day in Seattle, I decided I'd drink my coffee before finding my phone.

Ten minutes later I was sitting on the sofa, watching the ducks land on the glittering green water of Lake Union, and my first instinct was to take a picture. A shot like that would be good for at least 100 Facebook likes, probably a dozen retweets. But I remembered I was taking a break from my phone, so I settled into the cushions, took a deep breath, and sipped my coffee.

That's when I thought of Maria-something from last night. She was tall, just an inch or two shorter than me, and wore tight jeans and a UW sweatshirt. Cute as hell and definitely into me. We'd played darts and downed pints and ate sausage and laughed about people who eat kale salads.

It was all coming back to me. We'd ordered our Ubers side by side, then stood outside the pub in the warm midnight air as the crowd streamed out around us. When her car arrived, she'd leaned in and pecked me on the cheek. Her hair smelled like cloves and cinnamon.

I was struck by a sudden urge to see if she'd texted, along with an equally strong urge to scan her social media accounts to learn more about her. They say that Facebook is where we lie to our friends and Twitter is where we tell the truth to strangers, so I'd need to check them both. But first I needed to find my phone.

I started by checking all the same places I'd checked earlier. Kitchen counter, bedside table, jacket, sofa cushions, sheets and pillows. Next I checked under the bed, on top of the cabinet in the bathroom, under the sofa, and in all the pockets of everything I was wearing the night before.

I live in a small, but elegant, one-bedroom apartment in one of the new constructions built specifically for young techies like me. The design is clean and minimal, as are my furnishings. It only took me five minutes to check everywhere and by 9:30 I was back on the sofa, sipping my coffee and replaying the night in my head, trying to figure out where I'd left my phone.

The only two reasonable options were The Lion's Breath and the back seat of the Uber.

I grabbed my laptop and nestled back into the sofa. Seconds later, I was in my Uber account clicking "Connect via chat."

I'd slept off most of The Feeling and I was enjoying myself. I had Maria's number in my phone—a phone I couldn't find but soon would—the sun was out, the sofa cushions were soft and springy, the coffee was strong, and I could always check in on my accounts on my laptop, just to take the edge off.

A chat box popped up and, within a minute, I was connected to a representative named Billy.

Billy: How can I help you today?

Me: I think I left my phone in the car I got last night.

Billy: I'm sorry to hear that, how can I help you?

I'd assumed that my previous statement was self-explanatory. They must have a system for this, right?

Me: Did my driver report anything?

Billy: Oh, I'm sorry, we don't take reports of lost items. Please hold on while I find the information...

I waited, focusing in on the part of the chat box that said, "The agent is typing a response." Three little dots, like an ellipsis, refreshing over and over.

. . .
. . .
. . .

A minute went by. Then two.

. . .
. . .

16

. . .

The Feeling returned, this time in my shoulders. It was tension mixed with a crawling sensation, like spiders inside my designer t-shirt. I looked out at the water and took a sip of coffee. Everything was basically cool, life was good, but the longer I stared at those dots, the more I felt like something was wrong that could *never* be fixed.

. . .

. . .

. . .

I take yoga three days a week, mostly because my sister told me it would be a good way to meet women, so I took belly breaths like I'd learned in class. My shoulders relaxed a little, but then my head began to pound. Maybe I'd had one too many pints after all.

I breathed deeply into my heart, also like I'd learned in class, but all I felt was a buzzing irritation through my whole body.

. . .

. . .

. . .

The message finally popped up.

Billy: Please see the link below regarding how to contact your driver to retrieve your missing item.

https://help.uber.com/h/53539bde-f6f4-4909-85de-fa0b99f82be0

I clicked the link and closed the chat tab without saying goodbye.

The link explained that I needed to enter a phone number in a box. The system would then connect me directly to the driver's phone. Then I could ask about the phone or, at worst, leave a message. Of course, the page made sure to point out that: "Drivers are independent contractors. Neither Uber nor drivers are responsible for the items left in a vehicle after a trip ends. We're here to help, but cannot guarantee that a driver has your item or can immediately deliver it to you."

I had already entered the first five digits of my number when it hit me. I didn't have my cell phone.

I re-read the instructions, which I'd skimmed the first time around. "If you lost your personal phone, enter a friend's phone number instead."

I don't have a landline, so my first thought was to ask Gretchen, the website designer in the apartment next door. But her kitchen always smelled weird, like fermentation and incense. My head was throbbing and I just couldn't take that smell.

Then I had another idea, a two-birds-with-one-stone idea. Maria.

I logged onto Facebook, figuring I could find her through mutual friends. She seemed to know Miranda, a folk singer who pulled pints at The Lion's Breath on Saturday nights. Miranda had friended me six months ago, probably in hopes that I'd buy her self-produced album, which she pimped constantly on her feed in clear violation of Facebook's terms of service. But when the reassuring blue banner popped up, I realized that I wouldn't need to search for her after all.

Maria had sent me a friend request.

11 AM

After a brief chat on Facebook, during which I concealed my satisfaction at the fact that she had logged onto Facebook late last night to stalk my social media and friend me, we agreed to meet for brunch at Pepper's, an old-school diner I ate at when I wanted to rebel against the enviro-chic joints I was forced to eat at during business lunches.

On the walk over, I found myself calculating how long it would be until I had my phone back. Best-case scenario, I'd reach that yellow-toothed Uber driver and he'd drop it off at the diner in exchange for a big tip. Worst-case scenario, he wouldn't have it and I'd walk the mile or so to The Lion's Breath after a nice plate of corned beef hash.

But as I turned the corner and smelled the grease from Pepper's deep fryers wafting down the block, I started to have darker thoughts as well. What if the phone wasn't in either place? I paused at the diner's dented metal door, contemplating this.

Obviously, I'd just get a new phone. We designed The Feeling to be unbearable. We designed it so that you'd *have to* buy a new phone. I saw myself walking into the Apple Store, plopping down my Visa and returning home. I'd plug it into my laptop, download all my apps and contacts. Everything would be the same.

But I fucking hated the idea.

It felt like an episode of an old sitcom where the kid's hamster dies and the well-meaning, idiotic dad— probably played by Bob Sagat—tries to replace it before the kid comes home from school. I knew a new phone would have the same technology, but it wouldn't be *mine*. My thumb wouldn't feel the same on the home button, which we designed to soften about 2% over time. The case wouldn't have that yellow-gold stain from the time I did the turmeric lemonade cleanse. There wouldn't be that single particle of dust under the screen protector that's annoyed me continuously for six months but I still don't clean.

I knew how stupid these thoughts were while I was having them, but then I realized that they weren't thoughts at all. The Feeling was creeping back in. My mind knew that any iPhone was as good as any other. But that thing was part of my body. It was a blankie or a favorite stuffed animal. I needed it to feel okay, and I needed to get back to finding it.

Maria was stashed away at a booth in the far corner. She'd pulled her black hair into a ponytail, but she was even prettier than I remembered. She smiled broadly when she saw me and her dimples were so cute I almost took a step back. I hadn't planned to have a drink, but before I even sat down, she lifted up her Bloody Mary and said, "Hair of the dog. Want one?"

I nodded, thinking that as long as I didn't have my phone, I may as well have a drink.

The waiter was hovering nearby and Maria called out to him confidently. "Another round."

I slid into the red vinyl booth, pawing nervously at my hipster beard. "I lost my phone," I said.

She shot me a wrinkled-eyebrow look. "Nice to see you, too."

"Oh," I said, realizing how lame it was to sit down and mention my phone right out of the gate. "I meant—"

"I'm just messing with you. You already told me when we chatted. Remember?"

I was disoriented. I'd only stood at the door to the diner for a minute, but it was like I'd fallen into some foggy dream world.

"Right," I said, trying to play it cool. "Anyway, it's good to see you."

"You want to do the Uber thing now or—"

The waiter set down my drink and I took a long sip. The sweet-tart liquid went straight to my brain and everything got bright and clear. At that moment, all the shit about my phone seemed silly and far away.

"No," I said, "let's drink these first."

Noon

I read once that as hunter-gatherers transitioned into city-dwelling people, the first thing they did was to start making alcohol. The idea was that, if we're going to have laws and religions and societies—if we're going to *create civilization*—we're going to need a drink.

And after two Bloody Marys, I understood why. The Feeling was long gone, and life was good again. I was sitting with a smart, beautiful grad student who seemed genuinely interested in cell phone buttons, in iOS upgrades, and in what it's like having "a real job."

It turned out she was one semester away from getting her Master's in clinical psychology, and she'd clearly aced her class in "Asking Questions in a Neutral Tone That Lead the Client to Tell Deep Truths About Themselves."

As we paid our bill, I was telling her about the cupcake incident and the baseball glove and the day my parents gave away our beloved golden retriever because we were moving into Seattle from the suburbs.

"What was that like for you?" she asked, pulling the bill toward her and slapping down a credit card before I could stop her.

"I loved that dog and felt…"

The waiter came and took the credit card.

"Felt what?"

"Like there was just a hole in my life. We'd had him since before I was born and—"

"You hadn't known a world without him."

"Exactly."

I smiled down at the table and slowly raised my eyes to meet hers. She was smiling, too.

It sounds sappy, I know, but you have to understand that the whole thing was going down with a layer of irony. She was playing the role of therapist and I was playing the role of scarred little boy. I wasn't on the verge of tears or anything.

"Can we get out of here?" I asked.

"Don't we need to do that Uber thing?"

The moment she mentioned it, a knot formed in my stomach, but the Bloody Marys gave me enough courage to ignore it. "Totally. Can I use your phone?"

She slid her phone across the table. iPhone 7, same model as mine, and I remembered noticing it the night before. I opened Safari, found the Uber page I needed, then handed her the phone when the box popped up.

She entered her number and asked, "What now?" just as the phone started ringing. She handed it back to me and I put it on speaker phone.

I glanced around the diner. There was no one within a few booths of us, so I figured it wouldn't be too rude if I spoke quietly.

After three rings, a man's voice. "Hello?"

"Oh hi, thanks for picking up. I was in your car last night, around one."

"*One* is in the morning, not night."

Up until that point, all I'd remembered were the driver's yellow teeth and hideous smile, but now more memories were starting to flutter through. This guy was a smartass. I'd told him what I did for a living and he'd made sure to tell me that he was a "Samsung guy."

"Okay, early this morning," I said. "I think I left my phone in your car."

"Nope."

He sounded certain, dismissive, and eager to end the call. He'd spoken like this last night, with a directness and precision. Like he couldn't wait to get to the end of his words, so he sort of clipped them on the last syllable.

"I mean, can you at least check your—"

"I do a sweep of my vehicle at the end of every day. I often find phones, hair bands, lipstick cases. Sometimes a wallet. Last night I found nothing."

As he spoke, I was playing our interaction from the night before over and over in my head. I remembered how out-of-place he'd looked pulling up in his dark blue Toyota Prius. He'd rolled down the curbside window and leaned over and I'd noticed his ratty black t-shirt with the logo of some brand of cigarettes on it. He had long blond hair, not exactly a mullet, but something close. I remembered his crooked teeth, grinning at me in the rearview mirror as I swayed, pleasantly drunk, in the backseat. I try not to fall into in stereotypes, but he looked like he should have a thick Tennessee accent. Like he'd be more at home shotgunning beers at a NASCAR track than driving techies like me around Seattle.

"Look," I said, "is there any way you could check

again? I'm pretty sure it's there. Or can we meet so I can check through your car?"

"No one inspects my ride but me."

"I...I just..."

Something wasn't right, but I had no recourse. I looked at Maria, who was staring out the window. I couldn't even tell if she was listening.

"Okay," I said. "Thanks for nothing."

1 PM

At brunch, Maria had mentioned that she'd never been to Pike Place Market, despite being in grad school here for three years, so we'd taken the long route to The Lion's Breath. I'd managed to keep the knot in my stomach from growing by asking her all sorts of questions about psychology.

But the whole walk over, I couldn't stop thinking about the Uber driver. Did I really just have to take his word for it? He said he hadn't found my phone so...that's it? The more I thought about it, the more it bothered me.

When we stepped into The Lion's Breath, more of the night came back to me. I saw the exact stools we'd been sitting in, the third and fourth from the right along the wooden bar. I walked straight up to the bartender but Maria hung back by the door. I noticed that the further I got from her, and the closer I got to the bar, the denser the knot in my stomach became.

What if it wasn't there? Or what if I *had* left it there but someone had stolen it, wiped it clean, and already had it for sale on eBay?

I stood at the bar and tried to catch the bartender's

eye. He finished with another customer and called to me, "What'll ya have?"

"No, I'm looking for my phone. I think I left it here last night."

He sighed and walked to the cash register at the center of the bar, then dropped to one knee. "What kind?" he asked.

"iPhone seven. Simple white case. Finish of the phone is black. Not the jet black but the matte black. Tiny speck of dust in the top-left corner under the screen protector. Small yellow stain on the—"

He stood up and leaned on the bar just a couple feet from me. "Nothing."

"Nothing? I mean, can you check again?"

He just stared at me.

"It *has* to be there. Where the hell else could it be?"

"I'm sorry, it's not—"

"Someone took it."

He raised an eyebrow, but said nothing.

In retrospect, this is when I started to lose my shit. "Someone took it and I want the names of everyone who was tending bar here last night, everyone who—"

I felt a hand on my lower back and turned to see Maria.

"It's not here," she said, nodding toward the exit door. "Let's go."

I gave the bartender an angry look, but eased away when Maria slid her arm through mine and tugged gently toward the door.

2 PM

Maria and I sat on a bench in Westlake Park, shaded from the sun by the bright green leaves above us. I'd called Uber on the walk over, and they'd

25

confirmed what I already knew. If the driver said he didn't have my phone, there was nothing I could do.

I didn't want to lose it in front of Maria, so I'd thanked the representative respectfully and ended the call, then casually asked her about football, the great unifier. She was from North Carolina, so we could talk about the Seahawks-Panthers rivalry with a flirty intensity that worked for both of us.

After half an hour, she leaned in and took my hand, then scooched down the bench and put her head on my shoulder. The day had grown hot, but a cool breeze blew through the park and rustled the leaves. A low-hanging branch swayed in and out of my field of vision with the wind, giving me something to focus on instead of the yellow-toothed, mouth-breathing bastard who'd stolen my phone.

I watched the branch, and the couples with strollers passing through the bright sun on the walkway before us, and for a moment I was at peace.

Then I was struck by the urge to tweet something about it, and that brought me back to my phone. Facebook messages were probably piling up, and texts. What if my manager hadn't gotten those specs I sent him Saturday afternoon? Or what if something had happened to my mother?

I said, "Have you ever lost a phone?"

"I have."

"Did you feel terrible?"

"Not especially."

We sat in silence for a few minutes, then Maria said, "I did an internship with a hospice company last year. You know, health care for dying people. One of the patients who was dying of cancer would one day be happy to visit with friends and family and discuss worldly things, and the next day he'd have a faraway look in his eyes and not engage with anyone. The family asked why this was happening. I heard the nurse tell them it was the process of the soul leaving the body. She said that, as the soul practices leaving, a person will seem very far away. Touch and sound from loved ones will cause the soul to rejoin the body temporarily. A dying person will do this dance of separation back and forth until, ultimately, it becomes too painful for the soul to return to the confinement of the body. That's when death occurs."

It was a nice story, but I didn't get the point. "Not sure what you're getting at."

Her head was still on my shoulder and she glanced up at me. "I bet there was a moment today when you felt happier without your phone. Like you'd moved into a different realm, free and unconstrained."

I closed my eyes to think, trying to come up with something clever to say, but the knot had returned to my stomach. My shoulders tensed, even with Maria's head still resting on one of them. I kept seeing that driver grinning at me in the rearview mirror, and I was beginning to believe that I hadn't forgotten my phone at all.

Maybe I'd nodded off during the trip. Maybe he'd leaned back and swiped my phone while stopped at a light. Maybe his modus operandi was to work the late shift and pick up drunk people he could rob, people too out of it to notice until the next morning. Maybe he needed someone to teach him a lesson and—

"Hey."

I opened my eyes to find Maria standing over me. She'd gotten up without me noticing.

"Hey, what's going on?"

I looked down at my hands. My fists were clenched and shaking.

"What the hell is going on with you?"

"I...I just—"

"You got all tense and haven't responded to me in two minutes."

I consciously relaxed my hands, but I could still feel the knot in my stomach and the heat coursing through my chest. "I'm sorry."

She stared down at me for a few seconds, like she was making a decision. Finally, she said, "You have anger issues. You need help. I'm sorry, I'm outta here."

With that, she turned and walked away. Her shape was amazing and she had this walk that was a little more side-to-side than it needed to be, like her hips had a mind of their own. And it worked for her.

As I watched her go, I knew I'd screwed it up. The problem was, I didn't care.

11 PM

A dark blue car caught my eye, but as it approached I saw that it was a Ford Taurus.

I was outside The Lion's Breath wearing a form-fitting black t-shirt and skinny jeans, pacing casually like I was just waiting to meet up with some friends. But what I was really doing was watching the traffic. Priuses are everywhere in Seattle, but I knew the one I was looking for.

Getting a new phone hadn't been as bad as I thought. I just walked into the cathedral-like Apple store, told them what I wanted, asked them to assign my number to the new phone, and walked out.

A couple hours later, I was watching CNN on my couch while downloading my contacts, songs, podcasts, and bookmarks onto my new device. By the end of the process, I had what was essentially the same exact phone. I'd even gotten an identical white case.

But as I'd held it in my hand in the warm night air, pretending to read a text while glancing up occasionally at the passing cars, it didn't look right. There was no yellow stain on the case, no speck of dust under the screen protector. And worse than that, worst of all, this one had new idiosyncrasies that I was going to have to live with. The case had a tiny imperfection, a little nib of silicon at the seam on the middle-right, just where my ring finger hit when I wrapped my hand around it.

And that little nib was driving me fucking crazy.

So there I stood, in the shadow of the green awning of the fancy umbrella shop next to The Lion's Breath, waiting on that dark blue Prius. Sunday nights were slower than Saturdays, but there was a good crowd inside and a steady stream of people coming and going. And, of the ones who were going, many were hopping in Ubers.

I knew the chances were that he wouldn't show up that night. But I'd be back. I'd come back every night until I saw him. I'd wait there, under the awning, eyes trained at the street, and eventually he'd have to show up. I'd see the blue Prius pulling to a stop and I'd slide into the back seat before he knew what was happening.

Most likely he'd sold the phone already, but there was a chance he'd had it wiped and was using it himself. Maybe I'd even catch him tapping away on that beautiful little screen. Maybe he'd tried to clean the turmeric stain and, if I caught him with it, I'd tell him, "Jokes on you, dude, that thing is *never* coming out."

I'm not a violent person, but I'd grill him until he admitted it. And if he didn't, I'd wring his little neck.

A blue sedan pulled up and I held my breath for half a second. But it wasn't the Prius. Two young women popped out, laughing and already drunk, and stumbled into The Lion's Breath.

Midnight

Three Priuses had come and gone, and I was getting tired. I checked the time on my new phone, then turned to walk home. That's when I saw the driver.

But he wasn't behind the wheel of the Prius. He was half a block away, on the other side of The Lion's Breath, walking toward me.

I stepped back into the shadows and leaned against the building. It was clear he hadn't seen me from the way he was walking casually, stopping to glance into storefront windows along the way. If he'd seen me, he'd have looked guiltier, or maybe he'd have turned to run.

In any case, he was coming right at me. The lights from the storefronts sparkled off the grease in his shoulder-length blond hair, and I saw red. He was fifty yards away now, but I decided to wait, to see where he was headed.

Forty yards away.

Then thirty.

When he was just twenty yards away, a gang of

four couples streamed out of The Lion's Breath and I lost sight of him.

They paused to light cigarettes and I crept around them, still close against the building. All of a sudden, they moved in unison to cross the street and I saw the guy.

He was only about ten yards away and he stepped back when he saw me staring at him.

He was wearing an old-school "Save the Whales" t-shirt, the kind I saw all over when I was a kid, and this threw me off briefly.

But I clenched my fists and took three large steps toward him. "Hey!"

"Are you talking to me?"

"Yeah. You drove me last night."

He scanned me. "Are you the guy who lost his phone?"

I was trying to read his face, to figure out how far I was going to have to take this. "You *know* that I am."

"Did you find it?"

He was inching toward the door of The Lion's Breath, clearly wanting no part of me. His back was to me now and he was about to step into the pub.

"Excuse me," I said, grabbing his shoulder and spinning him around. "But you *know* I didn't find it."

He stepped back while brushing my hand off his shoulder. "What are you—"

"Give me my phone."

I was right up in his face. I had at least six inches on him and I could tell he was the kind of guy who wouldn't really fight back. I could smell cheap beer on his breath and see a little chip on one of his front teeth, which were even yellower than I remembered.

"Man, I don't know what—"

My phone vibrated in my back pocket.

"Bro," he said. "Your phone is vibrating. Why do you think—"

I pulled it out and held it a few inches in front of his nose. "This is my *new* phone. I spent six hundred dollars on it today."

As I pulled it away from his face, I read the caller ID: *Next Door Gretchen.*

I stared at it for a second and, as I did, the greaseball pulled away and darted into The Lion's Breath, probably figuring I wouldn't have the guts to kick the crap out of him in there. He was right about that, but I'd wait for him outside.

I stepped back into the shadow of the umbrella store, glancing around for an empty beer bottle or a stick to use as a weapon when he came out.

I swiped at my new phone. "Gretchen, I'm pretty busy. What's up?"

"That's weird. I guess you *didn't* lose your phone."

"What?"

"I thought I'd found your phone in the hallway, but if you're answering it, I must have found someone else's."

I clenched the new phone in my hand, trying to crush it. It was like she was taunting me. "My phone was *stolen.*"

"I could have sworn that your phone had a yellow stain from the time I convinced you to do that turmeric lemonade cleanse."

I opened my mouth, but nothing came out. Cars sped by, occasionally hitting me with a stream of headlights.

"Anyway, I found a phone on the landing between our apartments. Are you sure it's not yours?"

I watched through the window as the greasy-haired driver sipped a pint of dark brown beer. Old memories flooded through me again, but this time with a golden hue, like my whole past, every moment, had been made new. I shivered as a warm wind blew through my beard and dried the sweat on my face.

I tilted my head back slowly and looked up at the starless sky.

"Thank you," I managed to say. "Oh, Gretchen, thank you."

CELEBRITY-PRAYERS.NET

I had never prayed before. On TV, they kneel down—is it one knee or two?—and put their hands in some sort of triangle. Sometimes they make the sign of the cross.

So I got on one knee, paused, and looked over my shoulder across my room. Sprawling bamboo floors, king-size Tempur-Pedic, three-foot-tall talking R2D2. I'm rich, or at least my parents are. They're Harvard professors. Dad teaches economic history and mom teaches semiotics.

I got up and locked the door, then knelt again, this time under the window that looks onto our pool and patio. I heard my mom and dad laughing by the pool, but I knew they couldn't see up to my room.

I closed my eyes.

This'll never work, I thought. Rich white kids don't pray. Not when their mom teaches semiotics. Plus, you have to believe for it to work. Everybody knows that.

I opened my eyes, then closed them again. You're supposed to keep your eyes closed.

I made the sign of the cross, though I'm not sure whether I did it right.

"God?" I said.

I should tell you now, I don't believe in God. I believe in April Morgan's little white panties. I caught a look at them at tennis camp this summer. I believe in other girls, too, but mostly April Morgan.

So it's not like I had converted or anything, but school was three days away and I had never had a girlfriend. I believed in April Morgan, so I prayed.

"God? Um, I don't know if you're there. Look, today is my sixteenth birthday. All I want this year is April Morgan. You know her, right? And, I mean, if you're up there then you must have invented sex, so…"

This is stupid, I thought. You know how sometimes you can just tell something isn't going to work and you give up halfway through? This was one of those times.

I stood and banged my head on the light that hangs from my ceiling, then sat at my desk. I always bang my head on that light because I'm tall. Tall and skinny. My dad says I look like Kevin McHale when he was younger.

So I sat down and powered on my twenty-seven inch flatscreen and G5 quad-core. My friends watch porn all the time, but once I saw April Morgan at tennis camp, I decided to be faithful to her. I know it sounds stupid, but you'll understand when you see her.

I opened my desk drawer and took out two little round silver boxes. Are they still called boxes if they're metal? Anyway, I took a bump of Adderall, then one of Ritalin to smooth it out.

Don't be so surprised. If you'd had access to the drugs kids do today, you would have done the same thing. They say that Adderall produces the same chemical effect as amphetamines, but you're not gonna see me buying meth off some white trash loser from Southie. And my parents borrow each other's meds all the time, so they're never gonna notice if one or two go missing.

So I opened up Google and typed in "how to pray." I found a bunch of advice—have a conversation with God, a sincere heart, be humble and sincere. All that shit.

I know I seem like a spoiled-rich dirtball, but I'm really not. I'm smart as hell. I can tell you the difference between semantics and syntactics, or explain how the downfall of the Third Reich had more to do with economics than the American military. But the truth is, I don't give a shit about any of that. I only care about April Morgan and those panties. If you were ever sixteen, you'd understand.

Anyway, on page two of the search results I saw it: www.Celebrity-Prayers.net.

"Thank God," I said, as I clicked the link.

I scanned the site and knew right away that this was the answer. The headline across the top read: *In Need? Have Your Favorite Celebrity Pray for You*

Here's the idea. You pick a celebrity, fill out a

form, then the site contacts the celebrity, who has already signed up as a prayer provider. The celebrity can accept or reject your prayer request. If he accepts, you pay the site, the site pays the celebrity a cut, and the celebrity prays for you.

Awesome, right?

So I'm reading through the list of celebrities—mostly d-listers like Santana Bryant, former defensive end for the Patriots, Bunny Hops, some eighties porn star, and Sally Manning, a drummer from some seventies band I'd never heard of—and that's when the bumps hit me.

Adderall makes everything awesome, like your brain is a fire that's breathing love into the world. And big, like that love expands out in all directions. You know how they say that the universe is still expanding from the big bang? You ever imagine the way the edge of the universe feels? Adderall makes you feel like that.

And Ritalin makes things sharp and focused. So, imagine you're the edge of the universe, getting bigger and bigger, holding in all the planets, all the stars, and all the space in between. But then you can see it all with a clear, calm, crispness. Now you understand why I do it, right?

So, the bumps hit me, I looked back at the site, and then I saw him: Tyson Whittiker.

If you haven't heard of him, you haven't been watching enough reruns. He starred on *Fresh Faces*, that mid-nineties show about the black family that moves into the rich neighborhood in L.A. He was the kid with the catch phrases. He took famous lines from movies and put the word *freeesh* in there.

Pretty stupid, I know, but he came up with some

good ones. *Say hello to my freeesh face.* Scarface. Or, my favorite: *You can't handle the freeesh face.* Watching a nine-year-old black kid do Jack Nicholson never gets old.

I know it sounds lame. A rich white kid, sitting in a wood-paneled room, surrounded by bookshelves full of Saussure, Barthes, and Merleau-Ponty, watching reruns of a cheesy show that was on before he was born. I mean, the production values alone make the whole thing comical. But I didn't care. There was something about that kid. He just had this...*thing*. He seemed happy. Like he was invisible to himself.

Don't laugh. You'll get it soon.

So I stared at his photo for a minute, then clicked to look at the costs. Turns out, there were a bunch of options.

Package A was one remote prayer for $250. Package B was a week of daily prayers for $1,000. Package C was bundled with package B and included a video recording of the celebrity praying for you: $1,500. The packages went all the way up to F, which was an in-person prayer meeting.

My mind wobbled a bit and the screen got fuzzy, so I took another bump, this time just the Adderall. I heard my mom laughing by the pool. She and my dad are cool. They leave me alone and don't pay enough attention to notice when I borrow their pills.

Package F said "inquire for pricing," so I filled in my information and clicked "submit."

I turned off my computer and lay on my bed. I looked at the clock. School starts in sixty-two hours, I thought. Those fuckers better be quick.

The next part, I only found out later. But stories are supposed to have a structure, so here it is.

Tyson was walking out the door of his shitty apartment in Brooklyn Heights when his phone beeped.

He turned back in and looked around for the beep. His apartment was small, dark, and littered with Burger King wrappers and cigarette butts.

I mean, this guy had a fucked-up life. Plus, he'd gotten fat. I guess that happens when your career peaks when you're nine and you have to spend the rest of your life doing ridiculous celebrity appearances and getting booed off the stage at lame stand-up clubs.

So he found his phone and looked at his email:

From: Staff@Celebrity-Prayers.net
To: Tyson-Whittiker@hotmail.com
Subject: Prayer Request
Dear Mr. Whittiker,

We are pleased to inform you that your prayers have been requested at an in-person session in Cambridge, MA. The requested prayer date is Tuesday, September 3, 2013. The agreed upon price for the appearance is $4,500, of which you will receive 70%, or $3,150. To accept this prayer request, click here.

Sincerely,
Your Team at Celebrity-Prayers.net

Seriously, if you want to know how far a man has fallen, just look at where he gets his email.

From what he told me later, he read the email while sitting on his fucked-up couch. You know, threadbare, springs coming out of the cushions. Then he rummaged around on the coffee table, found a cigarette, and lit it. He told me later that he had smoked half of it before he realized it was covered in ketchup. I mean, how fucked up is that?

But I guess he must have accepted the prayer request, because I woke up around midnight when my phone and computer dinged at the same moment. I looked down at my phone—iPhone 5, by the way—and read: "Your prayer request has been accepted."

I could go on about this part. I could tell you how I paid the $4,500 plus airfare without telling my parents, how they bitched about it for five minutes, then went back to their offices. I could say how I arranged for a taxi to pick him up at the airport, how I stayed up until two the next morning watching Fresh Faces reruns. But I'd rather get to the good part, when Tyson showed up.

The doorbell rang. It was late Tuesday morning, the Tuesday after Labor Day. Last day of summer. Both parents at work.

Anyway, I was sitting at the computer when the doorbell rang. I ran out of my room, but stopped at the top of the stairs when I saw him through the glass in the top half of the door.

He didn't look like I thought he would. On the website, they showed a picture of him from when he was still a star. Now, he was old and fat. I mean, I guess he was only in his late twenties, but he looked older.

I walked down the stairs and opened the door. Tyson smelled like you'd burned a whole pack of cigarettes inside a Goodwill. I mean, who still smokes cigarettes?

Anyway, while I'm smelling him, he put on a stern face and said, "*I'll be back*...with my *freeesh* face." Then he looked right into my eyes and broke into a big smile. "Tyson Whittiker," he said. "You Devon?"

"Um, yeah." I shook his hand. "Come in."

The next hour or two were really awkward, and I'd rather not talk about them. Long story short, we sat by the pool, he drank a glass of my dad's vodka, and I pretended to go to the bathroom and popped a couple expired Vicodin from the time my mom herniated a disc. Then he asked me what I wanted to pray about.

The vicodin hadn't kicked in yet and I wished I'd snorted it.

"Girls," I said. "I mean, I guess."

I stared at the leaves drifting into the pool. Fall had come early and fall in Cambridge is like an explosion in a fancy leaf factory.

"Girls?"

"Yeah."

He put the vodka on the glass table, shaped like a yin-yang. "How old are you?" he asked.

"Sixteen. Sunday was my birthday."

"Cool," he said. "Happy birthday."

We both sat for a minute.

Finally, he looked over at me and smiled. "Bet you got one girl in particular in mind."

Vicodin is good if you're looking to mellow out. Makes your body all soft, like the world is giving you a warm bath. So right about then I was happy it was kicking in, because otherwise I might not have answered.

"April," I said. "April Morgan."

Tyson looked at me for a long time. I had no idea

what he was thinking, but I got nervous with how long he was looking at me. Reminded me of when my dad read my report card.

Finally, he said, "Hey, Devon. You smoke weed?"

I said, "All the time."

◆◆◆

The truth is, I had never smoked weed. I like to control my high, and who knows what you're gonna get when you buy weed off some skater loser in Fort Washington Park?

But what I said was, "All the time."

That's when he took off his shoe and pulled out a tightly folded plastic baggy that was taped under the flap.

"When are your parents getting home?" he asked.

"Late," I said. "They teach evening classes on Tuesday."

"You wanna toke?"

I didn't.

"Yeah, awesome," I said.

So I went into the kitchen and got a lighter—one of those long ones you use for pilot lights.

When I came back to the pool, Tyson looked up at me. "First, we pray," he said.

I couldn't tell if he was serious, but then he got down on both knees and closed his eyes. There he was, kneeling on the blue slate around our disappearing-edge pool, leaves floating down and the smoke of someone's backyard barbeque wafting around us.

After a few seconds, he opened his left eye and gestured for me to kneel down next to him. I looked around the yard—I mean, who wouldn't?—and knelt. I put my hands together in a double fist, like Tyson.

I closed my eyes and we were silent for at least a minute. I wasn't sure what I was supposed to be doing, and I was happy I'd hit that Vicodin, because I could feel my knees melting into the slate like blue marshmallow.

April Morgan came into my mind and a breeze blew and I smelled the barbeque smoke. You know how sometimes smoke smells like grease and sweet? In that moment, I was sure I loved her.

Then Tyson spoke.

"Dear Heavenly Father, we are so thankful for this opportunity to worship thee. We are thankful for this beautiful home, for the men who built it, and for your glory made manifest in the trees around us and the sky above us. And we pray, oh Heavenly Father, that thy Spirit be with those who are sick or afflicted. Please lead us, guide us, and direct us in the ways of truth and right and give to us the strength to help others along the way, that we may serve all men as we serve you. We ask for these things in the name of Jesus Christ."

He paused. "Amen."

I had never been around a real person praying. I don't know if it was the mellow of the Vicodin, the warmth of the early fall air, or what, but I have to admit that I felt something. I don't know how long I knelt there, but I didn't open my eyes until Tyson put his hands on my shoulders.

"Devon, the prayer is over," he said. "Let's blaze one."

It wasn't until a couple hours later, as we lay on the pink floaties in the center of the pool, looking up at the darkening sky, that I realized he hadn't mentioned April Morgan in the prayer.

In the movies, pot makes people say stupid shit, which is another reason I never wanted to do it. But that night, I'm telling you, it made us smarter, and somehow deeper, and I forgot pretty quickly that he hadn't mentioned April.

Anyway, we talked for a couple hours and, right before Tyson left, I was trying to explain semiotics to him. We were floating on our backs in the pool, and I was talking fast—heart racing, but not in a dangerous way. "Signs don't just 'convey' meanings. They constitute a medium in which meanings are constructed. Semiotics explains how meaning is not passively absorbed by a static consumer of meaning, but arises only in the active process of interpretation. That is, meaning is not *discovered*, but *created*."

Except for the pot, and the Vicodin, my mom would have been proud of me. I mean, I'd read all that stuff before, but I'd never been able to put it all together like that.

But Tyson didn't say anything for a long time. Finally, he paddled his floatie over to me and splashed some water on my feet. "You feel that?" he asked.

"Yeah."

"And you feel the way your brain is tingling, millions of little particles all floating around, dropping like snow, or like the confetti at the end of the Super Bowl?"

"Yeah," I said. "I feel it."

"Everything you just said is bullshit. Ain't no such thing as meaning or not meaning. None of that matters unless you're looking for it. You ever hear of Nisargadatta?"

I hadn't.

"He said something like, 'All your speculations about consciousness, they circulate in the consciousness about which they speculate.'"

I looked up at sky, black now, and watched a faint star appear in the blackness. I watched the sky and felt the floatie move across the little ripples in the pool and, for just a moment, I knew what he meant.

Then I forgot what he meant, forgot even what he'd said, but I didn't feel like talking about semiotics anymore.

The next day was the first day of school.

After we'd smoked the weed and floated in the pool, Tyson left for his hotel and I told him I'd meet him after school to ride with him to the airport. His agent had set him up a lunch appearance signing autographs for the Harvard comedy club, which was sad, but not as sad as smoking a cigarette covered in ketchup.

I didn't see April Morgan until third period. We're both smart as hell—I think I told you that already—so we're both in AP chemistry.

I was sitting at the long desk when she came in. She wore a white skirt with red flowers on it. I don't know what kind of skirt, but it was all flowy and loose. Not like the tennis skirt. Her red hair was tied in all sorts of loops and braids. Maybe she was in a hippie phase or something, but I didn't care, because she sat next to me and, even though she just stared at the dry erase board, I could feel a tingling between us.

Now, I have to admit, I wasn't thinking about the prayer at all, and I wasn't even thinking about Tyson. But now that I think back on it, the tingling kind of reminded me of what I felt when we prayed.

So, there she was and there I was, and when Mr. Frank came in, he made us lab partners. A bunch of other stuff happened, but the important thing is that he made us lab partners. Halfway into class we started an experiment, making alum out of aluminum. Basic stuff, right?

A little later, as I dumped the potassium hydroxide onto the aluminum scrap, she looked up at me.

"How's your backhand coming?" she asked.

I put the beaker down. "Good. How's yours?"

"Good," she said.

"Awesome."

She added a few milliliters of distilled water. "You look good," she said. "Did you get a lot of sun over the summer?"

I didn't know what to say. The truth was, I hadn't. I mean, I played tennis once a week, but mostly I sniffed Adderall and rocked out on the G5.

"Yeah," I said. "I've been swimming a lot. Folks have a place on the Vineyard." I still don't know why I said that.

"Cool," she said. "Hey, maybe we could play some day after school? Tennis, I mean."

They say that when you die your life flashes before your eyes, but sometimes a piece of it flashes before your eyes while you're still alive. What happened next seemed like a long time, but it wasn't. I flashed back to my room, trying to pray, looking up praying online, finding Tyson, smoking the weed, and floating in the pool.

In my head, I said, "Thank you, God."

To April, I said, "Cool. Yeah. That'd be awesome."

Tyson and I took the Silver Line to the airport. I guess I didn't need to see him off, but I wanted to tell him what happened with April.

He was quiet on the train. The truth is, I was quiet, too. You know how sometimes you really want to tell someone something but for some reason you don't? Like it's bubbling up from your toes into your belly and wanting to foam out your mouth, but instead it just sticks at the top of your throat? It was like that.

Finally, when we hit the Silver Line Way stop, the old lady next to us got off and we were alone in our row.

"I got her number," I said. "She wants to play tennis."

He was staring at the ads that lined the top of the subway car. He looked down at me slowly and his eyes were heavy.

"Oh yeah?" he said. "Nice. Nice work, Devon." He looked out the window but we were in the tunnel under the river so all he could have seen was black.

We were quiet for a few minutes and, when the train came out of the tunnel, I knew we were almost at the airport.

"What's wrong?" I asked. "Didn't you hear? It worked."

"I'm sad," he said, still staring out the window. He looked at me. "You think me praying had anything to do with you getting her number?"

"I don't know."

"Let me tell you something." He took my shoulders, and I remembered the night before, when he had taken them just after we prayed. "Don't ever become a celebrity, alright? Before you're famous it seems like you're gonna feel a certain way, a way that will fix everything. And it does at first. You feel this glow, this bigness. Like some light is always on and it's inside you.

"But then you realize that every person you meet is taking a bit of that light, like they're using it to light themselves, to ignite their own spark. And, for a while, that can feel good, too. Like you're helping to light the world. But then one day, you realize it's all gone and your own light is out. She didn't give you her number because of the prayer. Your spark got fanned. You lit up."

He took his hands off my shoulders.

I didn't respond, and a couple minutes later the train stopped at the airport and he got off. I watched him walk to the platform and I didn't follow him in. He waved, but he didn't smile. I could tell he wanted to be alone.

I thought about him on the train back to Cambridge. Each stop, people got on and got off. I looked at each one, too. I don't usually do that.

I don't know why I looked so close that day, but everyone looked gray—like wet ash—and that's when I knew he was right about that whole spark thing, but wrong about being a celebrity.

Deep down, I knew April didn't give me her number because of the praying. I'm not stupid. But what's wrong with going around and lighting people ablaze? A lot of us need it, right?

In the end, I don't care what he said. Celebrities are awesome, and sometimes you need fireworks to see the sky.

THE LAST DAY ON EARTH OF ZELTA JONES, STARWOMAN

The grits was good and smooth that mornin'. And the grease from the bacon was slickin' up the griddle for the eggs. Customers love bacony eggs.

I stood half-frozen, watchin' the yolks harden on a pair of over-mediums and listenin' to the crackles and sizzles and splutters.

Mr. Malcolm shouted across the kitchen, "Ella, quit starin' at them damn yolks. Last table of the shift and they been waitin' ten minutes."

I glanced up and evil-eyed Mr. Malcolm. He was an angular and bony man, probably weighed half of what Peg weighed. She was standin' next to him by the door that led into the dinin' room, smilin' at Mr.

Malcolm and smackin' her gum like always. I think the two of them might have been doin' things together in the walk-in after shifts, but that was none of my business.

I said, "Just a minute on them eggs, Mr. Malcolm."

"That yolk ain't the sun, ya know." Mr. Malcolm slapped an ashy hand on Peg's wide back and pointed at me. "Maybe if she focuses real hard she'll land on Mars or somethin'."

Peg laughed and they both walked into the dinin' room. Before the door swung closed all the way, I heard Mr. Malcolm talkin' to a customer, "Sorry for the wait. You *know* how Biscuit Hands is."

I'd heard it all before, so I just flipped the eggs.

Peg and Malcolm and the rest of them could make fun all they wanted. The thing you humans don't get about space travel is that you've already done it. And I don't mean the silly ships y'all took to the moon. I mean bodies of light movin' across the universe. Truth is, it happens all the time, and most of y'all reading this could do it if you wanted. You just can't remember how, and that's why I got sent here.

To remind you.

You might wonder why I didn't get sent to some big city full of universities and Yankees and Liberals. If you're gonna send someone to teach humans about space travel, why choose Blue Mountain, Alabama, population 485?

Truth is, I don't know. They'll never admit it back home, but I think it mighta been a screw-up. Maybe someone heard the name Blue Mountain and thought it sounded nice. Where I'm from, the billions of stars look like a blue mountain with red and white specs all around, just sparklin' in the sky. So maybe it was that.

Or maybe it's 'cause my boss is sweet on me and he knew I would like southern cookin'. I'll ask him when I get back, but I don't think he'll tell me.

Nothing against Blue Mountain. It's a nice enough little town. We got one road, two stores, and a diner. But 'round here people only care about family and Alabama football, so you can see why it was hard to get them to understand when I started tellin' them about space travel. Folks here are too ignorant to be learned anything about what they are.

And that's why I'm leavin' today. Papers will say I killed myself, but I know I'm just goin' home.

I plated the eggs with four strips of bacon and two of my famous biscuits from the warmer, then slid it into the window and dinged the bell. My shift was over, so I took off my apron and hung it on the hook by the screen door at the back of the diner.

Mr. Malcolm and Peg came back into the kitchen and waved at me. Six days a week at noon, for the last twenty-six years, I'd said, "See ya'll tomorrow."

But right then, I knew I wouldn't be back. I said, "Bye y'all."

Mr. Malcolm gave me a kind of funny look as he slid his hand into the back pocket of Peg's jeans.

"Bye, Ella," they said at the same time.

I took a last look around the kitchen, then walked out into a warm Alabama rain to get myself a hose.

For those who ain't already read about me, in Blue Mountain they call me Ella Jones, line cook at Malcolm's Diner. But my real name is Zelta Jones, Starwoman. Really, my name ain't Zelta, either. I'm just puttin' Zelta 'cause it's the closest word you got for the way my name makes you feel. Sexy and powerful both.

I come from a small system, just gettin' our legs under us. The older systems get all the good planets to look at, but we got Earth. No offense meant. I been one of you for forty-six years, but, by universal standards, you ain't shit. When I was first comin' up as a line cook, sometimes my gravy would get lumpy 'cause I wouldn't mix the cornstarch with water before I dumped it in. Mr. Malcolm would say, "Damn, Ella, looks like you dumped an outhouse in a cook pot." To a lot of systems out there, earth is like that.

But not to me. I love y'all.

Anyway, I got sent here forty-six years ago to help you folks, but for the first thirty of those years I forgot what I was supposed to be doing down here in the first place. See, some of the other systems—the *really* nice ones—can just visit here whenever they want. They developed themselves such that they can be in two places at once. So, while they're sittin' back at home, they can come down here, check in on you, abduct folks, *whatever.*

But we ain't there yet. We can't be in two places at once, so we have to do it the old-fashioned way, through a body. So that's how, forty-six years ago, I came to be in the womb of Myrtle Marie Jones, my mama.

When I was little, my mama told me that God had sent me to her and that I didn't have a daddy. But by the time I learned about sex, she admitted she'd been drunk in a bar and let some beer truck delivery guy make her acquaintance in the women's room.

So I was born and came up in Blue Mountain, Alabama, and didn't never know nothin' other than Main Street, my mama's cookin', our little white school house, and the blue mountain in the distance. After high school, I worked a couple odd jobs— deliverin' groceries to old folks and stockin' shelves at the Food Mart up in Anniston. I even went to college up in Tuscaloosa for half a semester, but it weren't for me. By age twenty I'd found my callin' on the grill at Malcom's. And for ten years, that's all I knew.

Four in the morning I showed up for biscuit prep. From the time I was five, I just had the feel for biscuits—overwork the dough and the biscuits get tough, underwork it and they fall apart—so folks said I had biscuit hands. We opened at five for the first of the loggers. Crack the eggs, keep the grits smooth, ladle the butter, plate it up with bacon or ham and a couple biscuits. Ding. Eight hours a day, six days a week for ten years I did that, but all of a sudden, somethin' didn't feel right.

Thirty years and fifty-two days after I came down here (I ain't countin' the nine months), I looked down at the griddle and somethin' was different.

I cracked the eggs and they sizzled just the same. I stirred the grits, but I found myself lookin' in the pot for a long time. I looked back at the eggs, but my timing was off. I ladled the butter and dropped some corn-cake batter, then went to flip the eggs, but I broke the yolks.

I used the spatula to throw them in the can next to the stove, but instead of going back to the griddle, I just stood there, starin' into the can. The thick black garbage bag was mostly empty, but I could see the whites at the bottom on a pile of coffee grounds. The yolks had splattered the sides of the bag. One big yellow-gold splotch and a bunch of little dots sprayed around it against the deep black of the bag.

That's when I remembered the stars and remembered who I was.

From the diner, I waddled south on Main Street. I walk like a duck because I'm almost as thick as I am tall. I know what you must be thinkin', but there ain't no shame in waddlin'. People spend a mess of time worryin' about being fat, but I never did 'cause I knew what I really was. Plus, where I'm from, we don't eat, so I thought I better enjoy it while I could.

I was headin' to Ancient Larry's store to get a hose, but when I slid up under his awnin' to get out of the rain, he said, "Closed today."

"Why?"

"Columbus Day."

"Then why are you settin' out front of your store just like regular?"

He smiled a crooked-toothed smile and picked at something in his teeth. "That's just what I do on Mondays."

"You see the game?"

Larry looked at me like I was even crazier than when I'd first told him about coming from another planet. He said, "What the hell else would I have been doing on Saturday?"

Larry had been friends with my mama before she died and, when I was a girl, he took me to my first game up in Tuscaloosa. He loved the Crimson Tide and, even though I didn't care about football one way or another, around here you pretended or you got run outta town.

So he took me up to the game and I cheered every time he did, but mostly I took in the spectacle of the whole thing. Ninety-thousand people, all that energy and emotion, the stadium shaking. My heart damn near beat out of my chest that day. That's one thing we ain't got where I come from: hearts beatin' out of chests.

I said, "Roll Tide."

"Roll Tide," he said. "What you need, anyway?"

"Hose."

"What fer? Ain't gardenin' season."

"Just need one."

He wiped his hand across his face and looked right at me. "Something peculiar about you today. Always has been but today it's more."

"How you figure?"

"Well there's all that space stuff you started talking a while back. But it was there before that. You ain't seem like you from Alabama."

"I *ain't* from Alabama." The rain started comin' a little harder and I slid closer to him under the awning. "Any chance you'll get me a hose, even though you closed?"

"If you tell me what's it fer."

I looked at him long and hard for near a minute. It's weird lookin' at someone who doesn't know where they come from.

For the first few weeks after the whole egg in the garbage thing, I could still remember what it was like to not remember what I was. And sometimes I would even forget altogether. I'd go back to how I was before I remembered. Like the time Mean Joe kept sendin' back my grits, saying they were lumpy, but they weren't. After he sent them back a third time, I went out and dumped a bowl of buttery grits right on his head.

Later that night, I thought, "Ain't that funny. I mistook myself for a lady who makes grits." But after a while I just forgot all about it and sometimes I forgot that other people had forgot, too.

Anyway, standin' there and starin' at Ancient Larry, I felt sad for the first time in a long time, and I didn't know what to say.

He must've got uncomfortable with the starin', 'cause he said, "So, you gonna tell me?"

"I aim to kill myself today. Gonna use the hose to carry the tailpipe fumes into my truck. Saw it on TV."

I don't know why I told him. Maybe I didn't want to tell a lie on my last day on Earth. Maybe it was because, even where I come from, you're supposed to respect your elders. Or maybe it was because he took me to that football game or because, of all the people in town, he was the only one who never made fun of me when I started tellin' everyone they could space travel.

He smiled at first, then his face went kinda blank. "Why? I mean, ain't that the easy way out?"

I couldn't tell if he knew I was serious, if he was humorin' me, or if he was just talkin' to talk without knowin' one way or another. He was used to me sayin' weird things, so my guess is he thought I was messin' around.

I said, "Ain't gon' be all that easy if you won't sell me a hose." He smiled and I smiled back. "Plus, how you know it's the easy way out if you ain't never done it yourself?"

He looked away and kinda scanned the road, but nothin' was happenin' worth lookin' at, so after a few seconds he looked back up at me. He said, "Why you think you so special, Ella? We all just come here from somewhere or other, then we go home when God calls us. Ain't up to us to decide. Even if what you said is true, even if you was from some other place, some other planet, they must have a God there like we do. Doesn't give you any right to decide to end it."

"Ain't ending nothin'."

"What if you wrong?"

"I ain't."

"What if you crazy?"

"I ain't."

He shifted in his chair and sorta rocked back and forth for a minute. That was his thinkin' posture. Usually he was thinkin' about the team, but I got the sense that he was thinkin' about me. I also got the sense that he wasn't gonna give me a hose.

"Just tell me straight out, no mumbo jumbo about space and whatever. Why you gonna do a thing like that?"

I shrugged. "Time to go home."

After what seemed like a long time, Ancient Larry broke out into a thin little grin. The grin grew and grew until finally he burst out laughing like I'd said the funniest thing he'd ever heard.

After about a minute of laughin', he said, "You crazy. You know you crazy, right?"

I didn't say anythin', but I guess he'd decided I wasn't serious, because he stood real slow and turned toward the door.

As he unlocked it, he turned back and scanned me, head to toe, then back up again. He let his eyes rest on my face for a long time. His eyes were black and twinkling and, for a moment, I felt like I was starin' down into that black garbage bag at that splatter of egg yolks, or like I was lookin' into a starry sky on a cold winter night.

For just a sec, I started to wonder whether I was doing the wrong thing. But then he stepped into the store and, a minute later, he came back with a twenty-five-foot green hose.

I left the hardware store and got in my truck, which I'd parked a little way down the block from the diner. I was headed to the Blue Mountain Quarry.

I turned on the radio to listen to some music, but I stopped between stations when I heard that cracklin' static sound. As I drove, I tuned my ears to the static and just let it fill me. In movies, people are always tryin' to find extra-terrestrial life through sound transmission, findin' patterns in the static, that kind of thing. For a while, watchin' those fools turn dials made me mad. Like why couldn't people just look harder at what they were? Why couldn't they realize that they could go there whenever they wanted if they trained themselves right? Why'd they have to go searchin' in some noise from outer space?

I drove past the Oakridge Baptist Church and the Wendell Hill Presbyterian Church and, as I left town, I turned the dial. Most of what we get in Blue Mountain is country, but there's also LOVE FM, the Christian station, and WROQ, the college station out of Birmingham.

I stopped on WROQ because I liked the sound of

the DJ's voice. He was talkin' about the game, so I tuned out his words and focused on his excited, optimistic tone. Young people give me hope sometimes. Even though the world around them went dark already, some of them still have a chance. Like if they can make it into their twenties without losing their minds, maybe they can figure out for themselves what I figured out.

A song came on, the kind of thing Mr. Malcolm would never let us listen to at the diner. The kid said it was by some band called *The Killers* and it started slow and low with a little dance beat. A few seconds later, a male singer came on and started talkin' about lettin' go and walkin' through open doors and cuttin' the cord and findin' the answer and all that kinda stuff.

His voice had a yearnin' in it, like he was wantin' to know somethin' so bad but just couldn't figure it out. When I was in my twenties, I walked around like most people, pretendin' to know a bunch of things I didn't know. But when I was alone in the bathtub, or under the covers at night, I'd have to admit to myself that I didn't know anythin' and then I'd just cry and cry.

Nothin' hurts more than feelin' a question, feelin' how big the mystery is, then lookin' out at a world of wrong answers to wrong questions. Nothing is lonelier than lyin' in bed at night with all these questions, lookin' for the answers and knowin' no one around you is even askin' the same ones. All anyone seemed to be askin' was whether Saban would have the boys ready for Saturday, whether the D-line could get to the new Auburn quarterback. But this guy, in this song, I could tell that at least he was askin' the right questions.

But it wasn't until the chorus of the song that I started to really *feel* him. He said, "Are we human or are we dancer?"

Just like that. Came out of the crummy speakers in my busted-up pickup truck that was almost as old as me, and I couldn't believe what I was hearin'. I listened close, kinda leaned into the speaker to the right of the steerin' wheel. Kept my left eye on the road. At first I thought he said "dancers." But the second and third time the chorus came around I knew he was saying *dancer*, no *s*. Like "dancer" was some kind of separate species, different than and probably more divine than humans.

That's when I thought maybe I had a soul mate. Maybe this guy was like me. Maybe he knew what I knew and he was tryin' to tell everyone like I had.

I can't even move my body as fast as that beat was playing, but it made my heart hot. Like a bunch of bodies smashin' into each other, all sweat and meat and love. Kinda reminded me of that day with Ancient Larry up in Tuscaloosa, actually.

As I pulled up to the quarry, my chest was poundin' and tears were drippin' from my eyes and I felt like my heart might explode. Then the beat faded and the DJ was back, talkin' about next week's matchup against Arkansas.

I turned off the radio and got out of the truck.

The quarry ain't much of a quarry, actually.

Alabama Stone bought up the land when I was a girl, thinkin' they'd tear it up and haul out the quartzite. But I guess they never found much because they dug up a long, thin sliver of earth, fenced it in, and never came back. Now it looks like a crack in the ground, maybe fifty feet wide, a couple hundred feet long and a couple hundred feet deep.

The rain had stopped and, as I got out of the truck, hundreds of birds rose out of the quarry as one, straight up like they were hoverin', then moved over my head and kind of stayed there for a half-second. They turned all together and flew north and I leaned on the fence, watchin' them until they disappeared over the trees.

For some reason, watchin' those birds made me think of Ancient Larry and my mama and Mr. Malcolm and Peg, and even Mean Joe, but nothin' in any of that made me think any different about what I was doin'. That song was still in my head, though, and it made me feel like I should stick around and go find that singer, whoever he was. Like maybe he and I could be friends and I wouldn't be so lonely here anymore.

But then I thought about home, about the billions of blue and red and white stars. I could feel myself leavin' already. I'd travel like light across galaxies and be home before my body was cold down here on Earth.

I opened the passenger door and grabbed the hose.

It only took a minute to set it up. I slid the hose into the tail pipe, then sealed it off with some duct tape I kept in the glove compartment. I ran the hose around the truck and into the passenger side window, then rolled up the window, leavin' about an inch of space. I sealed the space with more duct tape.

Ten minutes after pullin' up to the quarry, I started the truck.

I'd read up on the process in advance. Newer cars have emissions rules, but in my forty-year-old truck with a tiny cab, things would go quickly. Carbon dioxide is odorless and death is painless. Worst thing I read about it was that sometimes people panic for a moment when they stop breathin', but I doubted I'd do that because I knew where I was headed.

I reclined the seat and closed my eyes. The truck was shaking a little, like it always did when runnin'. I had my mind set on those stars, red and blue and white, twinklin' and twinklin'. I could see them in my mind and I knew I would be back to them soon.

After a minute, I got drowsy and kinda sunk into the seat.

I was still thinkin', though, thinkin' about my gravestone. I'd left a note on my kitchen table to let people know what had happened. All it said was, "I killed myself. Please put 'Ella Jones' on my gravestone." I left it with $1,000 I'd saved up from the diner.

Anyone who knows me by that name will probably remember me fondly. They'll remember my biscuit hands and say what a damn shame it was that I somehow got it twisted. Unless you've hurt them, people usually like to remember the good stuff. But as I was fadin', I was thinkin' about that singer. Maybe he would hear about me and come find my grave and understand. Maybe he'd look at it and see blue stars and red stars, twinklin' on the stones, and know the real me: Zelta Jones, Starwoman.

I felt myself leavin' my body, risin' up out of the truck, and I saw the blue mountain, stars and all. They were flashin' at me, welcomin' me home, and I knew I'd done the right thing. Soon I'd be talkin' with my old friends, tellin' them all about Earth and how no one down here knows anythin', but it's okay because they've got football and biscuits and this one guy in this one band who might be onto somethin'.

Blue and red and white.

Flashin'.

Flashin'.

Then I heard a voice. "That's her. Open it."

It was Ancient Larry and, for the briefest moment, I was happy. He'd come with me somehow. I felt it as a flash in my heart. Ancient Larry had come home with me and now I could show him things from *my home*, like he'd done with me.

I heard the door open and felt a rush of cool air.

"Ella!" Larry's voice again.

Then a different voice. "Grab her shoulders."

It was Bill Johnston, the sheriff, and almost before he'd finished speakin' I felt his massive hands under my arms, pullin' me out of the truck. Next thing I knew I was on the ground, a sharp rock pokin' into my right shoulder. The piercing pain kinda woke me up, and I opened my eyes slowly to see the red and blue lights of Sheriff Johnston's patrol car flashin' off the fence around the quarry.

Ancient Larry was on one knee and he leaned over me so his head was just about a foot from my own. His dark face was blurry and kind of runnin' into the sky, the two morphin' together so I couldn't tell where he stopped and the sky began. I had all kinds of thoughts runnin' through my mind, but mostly I was disappointed I'd have to go to work the next day.

Then Ancient Larry's face came into focus and I

saw the sparks in his eyes—blue and red and white—
and I forgot all about work.

He shook his head at me like he had a hundred
times when I'd said a hundred different crazy things.
"You already home," he said. "Dammit, girl, don't you
know you already home?"

THANKS FOR READING!

I'll be honest. Besides my family, nothing makes me happier than the thought of a reader finishing one of my books.

So...thank you!

As an indie author, I work hard to bring you excellent work as fast as I can. I've got *many* books in the works and I plan to be at this a long time. I hope you'll come along for the ride.

The best way to do that is by joining my reader club at: www.acfuller.com/readerclub

I never sell or rent your email address. I never send spam or junk, but I do send:

- inside information about my books
- invitations to in-person launch parties
- notes about my writing workshops
- recipes
- free books

I hope you enjoyed the stories and I look forward to hearing from you.

A.C. Fuller

Hansville, Washington

MY OTHER BOOKS

In addition to writing stories, I write novels. I call them "Media Thrillers" because they're fast-paced and set in the world of journalists and other media figures.

Here's the series list as it now stands:

The Cutline (An Alex Vane Novella)

The Anonymous Source (An Alex Vane Media Thriller, Book 1)

The Inverted Pyramid (An Alex Vane Media Thriller, Book 2)

The Mockingbird Drive (An Alex Vane Media Thriller, Book 3)—Coming in June, 2017

Find all my books by searching for "A.C. Fuller" on Amazon.

ABOUT THE AUTHOR

A.C. Fuller writes media thrillers and literary fiction. He's the creator and host of the WRITER 2.0 Podcast, a weekly interview show featuring award-winning writers and publishing experts.

He was once a freelance journalist in New York and taught in the NYU Journalism School from 2006 to 2008. He now teaches English at Northwest Indian College near Seattle and leads writing workshops around the country and internationally, including classes for the Pacific Northwest Writers Association, the Write in the Harbor Conference, and the Royal City Literary Arts Society.

He lives with his wife, two children, and two dogs near Seattle. Find out more at acfuller.com.

Made in the USA
San Bernardino, CA
11 April 2017